Essays on Paul Bourget

Mark Twain (Samuel Clemens)

Contents

ESSAYS ON PAUL BOURGET

BY

Mark Twain (Samuel Clemens)

WHAT PAUL BOURGET THINKS OF US

He reports the American joke correctly. In Boston they ask, How much does he know? in New York, How much is he worth? in Philadelphia, Who were his parents? And when an alien observer turns his telescope upon us--advertisedly in our own special interest--a natural apprehension moves us to ask, What is the diameter of his reflector?

I take a great interest in M. Bourget's chapters, for I know by the newspapers that there are several Americans who are expecting to get a whole education out of them; several who foresaw, and also foretold, that our long night was over, and a light almost divine about to break upon the land.

>"His utterances concerning us are bound to be weighty and well timed."

>"He gives us an object-lesson which should be thoughtfully and profitably studied."

These well-considered and important verdicts were of a nature to restore public confidence, which had been disquieted by questionings as to whether so young a teacher would be qualified to take so large a class as 70,000,000, distributed over so extensive a schoolhouse as America, and pull it through without assistance.

I was even disquieted myself, although I am of a cold, calm temperament, and not easily disturbed. I feared for my country. And I was not wholly tranquilized by the verdicts rendered as above. It seemed to me that there was still room for doubt. In fact, in looking the ground over I became more disturbed than I was before. Many worrying questions came up in my mind. Two were prominent. Where had the teacher gotten his equipment? What was his method?

He had gotten his equipment in France.

Then as to his method! I saw by his own intimations that he was an Observer, and had a System that used by naturalists and other scientists. The naturalist collects many bugs and reptiles and butterflies and studies their ways a long time patiently. By this means he is presently able to group these creatures into families and subdivisions of families by nice shadings of differences observable in their characters. Then he labels all those shaded bugs and things with nicely descriptive group names, and is now happy, for his great work is completed, and as a result he intimately knows every bug and shade of a bug there, inside and out. It may be true, but a person who was not a naturalist would feel safer about it if he had the opinion of the bug. I think it is a pleasant System, but subject to error.

The Observer of Peoples has to be a Classifier, a Grouper, a Deducer, a Generalizer, a Psychologizer; and, first and last, a Thinker. He has to be all these, and when he is at home, observing his own folk, he is often able to prove competency. But history has shown that when he is abroad observing unfamiliar peoples the chances are heavily against him. He is then a naturalist observing a bug, with no more than a naturalist's chance of being able to tell the bug anything new about itself, and no more than a naturalist's chance of being able to teach it any new ways which it will prefer to its own.

To return to that first question. M. Bourget, as teacher, would simply be France teaching America. It seemed to me that the outlook was dark--almost Egyptian, in fact. What would the new teacher, representing France, teach us? Railroading? No. France knows nothing valuable about railroading. Steamshipping? No. France has no superiorities over us in that matter. Steamboating? No. French steamboating is still of Fulton's date--1809. Postal service? No. France is a back number there. Telegraphy? No, we taught her that ourselves. Journalism? No. Magazining? No, that is our own specialty. Government? No; Liberty, Equality, Fraternity, Nobility, Democracy, Adultery the system is too variegated for our climate. Religion? No, not variegated enough for our climate. Morals? No, we cannot rob the poor to enrich ourselves. Novel-writing? No. M. Bourget and the others know only one plan, and when that is expurgated there is nothing left of the book.

I wish I could think what he is going to teach us. Can it be Deportment? But he experimented in that at Newport and failed to give satisfaction, except to a few. Those few are pleased. They are enjoying their joy as well as they can. They confess their happiness to the interviewer. They feel pretty striped, but they remember with reverent recognition that they had sugar between the cuts. True, sugar with sand in it, but sugar. And true, they had some trouble to tell which was sugar and which was sand, because the sugar itself looked just like the sand, and also had a gravelly taste; still, they knew that the sugar was there, and would have been very good sugar indeed if it had been screened. Yes, they are pleased; not noisily so, but pleased; invaded, or streaked, as one may say, with little recurrent shivers of joy--subdued joy, so to speak, not the overdone kind. And they commune together, these, and massage each other with comforting sayings, in a sweet spirit of resignation and thankfulness, mixing these elements in the same proportions as the sugar and the sand, as a memorial, and saying, the one to the other, and to the interviewer: "It was severe--yes, it was bitterly severe; but oh, how true it was; and it will do us so much good!"

If it isn't Deportment, what is left? It was at this point that I seemed
to get on the right track at last. M. Bourget would teach us to know
ourselves; that was it: he would reveal us to ourselves. That would
be an education. He would explain us to ourselves. Then we
should understand ourselves; and after that be able to go on more
intelligently.

It seemed a doubtful scheme. He could explain us to himself--that would
be easy. That would be the same as the naturalist explaining the bug to
himself. But to explain the bug to the bug--that is quite a different
matter. The bug may not know himself perfectly, but he knows himself
better than the naturalist can know him, at any rate.

A foreigner can photograph the exteriors of a nation, but I think that
that is as far as he can get. I think that no foreigner can report its
interior--its soul, its life, its speech, its thought. I think that a
knowledge of these things is acquirable in only one way; not two or four
or six--absorption; years and years of unconscious absorption; years
and years of intercourse with the life concerned; of living it, indeed;
sharing personally in its shames and prides, its joys and griefs,
its loves and hates, its prosperities and reverses, its shows and
shabbinesses, its deep patriotisms, its whirlwinds of political passion,
its adorations--of flag, and heroic dead, and the glory of the national
name. Observation? Of what real value is it? One learns peoples through
the heart, not the eyes or the intellect.

There is only one expert who is qualified to examine the souls and the
life of a people and make a valuable report--the native novelist. This
expert is so rare that the most populous country can never have fifteen
conspicuously and confessedly competent ones in stock at one time.
This native specialist is not qualified to begin work until he has
been absorbing during twenty-five years. How much of his competency is
derived from conscious "observation"? The amount is so slight that it

counts for next to nothing in the equipment. Almost the whole capital
of the novelist is the slow accumulation of unconscious
observation--absorption. The native expert's intentional observation
of manners, speech, character, and ways of life can have value, for the
native knows what they mean without having to cipher out the meaning.
But I should be astonished to see a foreigner get at the right meanings,
catch the elusive shades of these subtle things. Even the native
novelist becomes a foreigner, with a foreigner's limitations, when he
steps from the State whose life is familiar to him into a State
whose life he has not lived. Bret Harte got his California and his
Californians by unconscious absorption, and put both of them into his
tales alive. But when he came from the Pacific to the Atlantic and tried
to do Newport life from study-conscious observation--his failure
was absolutely monumental. Newport is a disastrous place for the
unacclimated observer, evidently.

To return to novel-building. Does the native novelist try to generalize
the nation? No, he lays plainly before you the ways and speech and life
of a few people grouped in a certain place--his own place--and that is
one book. In time he and his brethren will report to you the life and
the people of the whole nation--the life of a group in a New England
village; in a New York village; in a Texan village; in an Oregon
village; in villages in fifty States and Territories; then the farm-life
in fifty States and Territories; a hundred patches of life and groups
of people in a dozen widely separated cities. And the Indians will be
attended to; and the cowboys; and the gold and silver miners; and the
negroes; and the Idiots and Congressmen; and the Irish, the Germans, the
Italians, the Swedes, the French, the Chinamen, the Greasers; and the
Catholics, the Methodists, the Presbyterians, the Congregationalists,
the Baptists, the Spiritualists, the Mormons, the Shakers, the Quakers,
the Jews, the Campbellites, the infidels, the Christian Scientists, the
Mind-Curists, the Faith-Curists, the train-robbers, the White Caps, the
Moonshiners. And when a thousand able novels have been written, there

you have the soul of the people, the life of the people, the speech of the people; and not anywhere else can these be had. And the shadings of character, manners, feelings, ambitions, will be infinite.

> "'The nature of a people' is always of a similar shade in its
> vices and its virtues, in its frivolities and in its labor.
> 'It is this physiognomy which it is necessary to discover',
> and every document is good, from the hall of a casino to the
> church, from the foibles of a fashionable woman to the
> suggestions of a revolutionary leader. I am therefore quite
> sure that this 'American soul', the principal interest and the
> great object of my voyage, appears behind the records of
> Newport for those who choose to see it."--M. Paul Bourget.

[The italics ('') are mine.] It is a large contract which he has undertaken. "Records" is a pretty poor word there, but I think the use of it is due to hasty translation. In the original the word is 'fastes'. I think M. Bourget meant to suggest that he expected to find the great "American soul" secreted behind the ostentatious of Newport; and that he was going to get it out and examine it, and generalize it, and psychologize it, and make it reveal to him its hidden vast mystery: "the nature of the people" of the United States of America. We have been accused of being a nation addicted to inventing wild schemes. I trust that we shall be allowed to retire to second place now.

There isn't a single human characteristic that can be safely labeled "American." There isn't a single human ambition, or religious trend, or drift of thought, or peculiarity of education, or code of principles, or breed of folly, or style of conversation, or preference for a particular subject for discussion, or form of legs or trunk or head or face or expression or complexion, or gait, or dress, or manners, or disposition, or any other human detail, inside or outside, that can rationally be generalized as "American."

Whenever you have found what seems to be an "American" peculiarity, you have only to cross a frontier or two, or go down or up in the social scale, and you perceive that it has disappeared. And you can cross the Atlantic and find it again. There may be a Newport religious drift, or sporting drift, or conversational style or complexion, or cut of face, but there are entire empires in America, north, south, east, and west, where you could not find your duplicates. It is the same with everything else which one might propose to call "American." M. Bourget thinks he has found the American Coquette. If he had really found her he would also have found, I am sure, that she was not new, that she exists in other lands in the same forms, and with the same frivolous heart and the same ways and impulses. I think this because I have seen our coquette; I have seen her in life; better still, I have seen her in our novels, and seen her twin in foreign novels. I wish M. Bourget had seen ours. He thought he saw her. And so he applied his System to her. She was a Species. So he gathered a number of samples of what seemed to be her, and put them under his glass, and divided them into groups which he calls "types," and labeled them in his usual scientific way with "formulas"--brief sharp descriptive flashes that make a person blink, sometimes, they are so sudden and vivid. As a rule they are pretty far-fetched, but that is not an important matter; they surprise, they compel admiration, and I notice by some of the comments which his efforts have called forth that they deceive the unwary. Here are a few of the coquette variants which he has grouped and labeled:

THE COLLECTOR.
THE EQUILIBREE.
THE PROFESSIONAL BEAUTY.
THE BLUFFER.
THE GIRL-BOY.

If he had stopped with describing these characters we should have been obliged to believe that they exist; that they exist, and that he has seen them and spoken with them. But he did not stop there; he went further and furnished to us light-throwing samples of their behavior, and also light-throwing samples of their speeches. He entered those things in his note-book without suspicion, he takes them out and delivers them to the world with a candor and simplicity which show that he believed them genuine. They throw altogether too much light. They reveal to the native the origin of his find. I suppose he knows how he came to make that novel and captivating discovery, by this time. If he does not, any American can tell him--any American to whom he will show his anecdotes. It was "put up" on him, as we say. It was a jest--to be plain, it was a series of frauds. To my mind it was a poor sort of jest, witless and contemptible. The players of it have their reward, such as it is; they have exhibited the fact that whatever they may be they are not ladies. M. Bourget did not discover a type of coquette; he merely discovered a type of practical joker. One may say the type of practical joker, for these people are exactly alike all over the world. Their equipment is always the same: a vulgar mind, a puerile wit, a cruel disposition as a rule, and always the spirit of treachery.

In his Chapter IV. M. Bourget has two or three columns gravely devoted to the collating and examining and psychologizing of these sorry little frauds. One is not moved to laugh. There is nothing funny in the situation; it is only pathetic. The stranger gave those people his confidence, and they dishonorably treated him in return.

But one must be allowed to suspect that M. Bourget was a little to blame himself. Even a practical joker has some little judgment. He has to exercise some degree of sagacity in selecting his prey if he would save himself from getting into trouble. In my time I have seldom seen such daring things marketed at any price as these conscienceless folk have worked off at par on this confiding observer. It compels the conviction that there was something about him that bred in those speculators a quite unusual sense of safety, and encouraged them to strain their powers in his behalf. They seem to have satisfied themselves that all he wanted was "significant" facts, and that he was not accustomed to examine the source whence they proceeded. It is plain that there was a sort of conspiracy against him almost from the start--a conspiracy to freight him up with all the strange extravagances those people's decayed brains could invent.

The lengths to which they went are next to incredible. They told him things which surely would have excited any one else's suspicion, but they did not excite his. Consider this:

> "There is not in all the United States an entirely nude statue."

If an angel should come down and say such a thing about heaven, a reasonably cautious observer would take that angel's number and inquire a little further before he added it to his catch. What does the present observer do? Adds it. Adds it at once. Adds it, and labels it with this innocent comment:

> "This small fact is strangely significant."

It does seem to me that this kind of observing is defective.

Here is another curiosity which some liberal person made him a present of. I should think it ought to have disturbed the deep slumber of his suspicion a little, but it didn't. It was a note from a fog-horn for strenuousness, it seems to me, but the doomed voyager did not catch it. If he had but caught it, it would have saved him from several disasters:

> "If the American knows that you are traveling to take notes, he is interested in it, and at the same time rejoices in it, as in

a tribute."

Again, this is defective observation. It is human to like to be praised;
one can even notice it in the French. But it is not human to like to
be ridiculed, even when it comes in the form of a "tribute." I think a
little psychologizing ought to have come in there. Something like this:
A dog does not like to be ridiculed, a redskin does not like to be
ridiculed, a negro does not like to be ridiculed, a Chinaman does not
like to be ridiculed; let us deduce from these significant facts this
formula: the American's grade being higher than these, and the chain-of
argument stretching unbroken all the way up to him, there is room for
suspicion that the person who said the American likes to be ridiculed,
and regards it as a tribute, is not a capable observer.

I feel persuaded that in the matter of psychologizing, a professional
is too apt to yield to the fascinations of the loftier regions of that
great art, to the neglect of its lowlier walks. Every now and then, at
half-hour intervals, M. Bourget collects a hatful of airy inaccuracies
and dissolves them in a panful of assorted abstractions, and runs the
charge into a mould and turns you out a compact principle which will
explain an American girl, or an American woman, or why new people yearn
for old things, or any other impossible riddle which a person wants
answered.

It seems to be conceded that there are a few human peculiarities that
can be generalized and located here and there in the world and named
by the name of the nation where they are found. I wonder what they are.
Perhaps one of them is temperament. One speaks of French vivacity
and German gravity and English stubbornness. There is no American
temperament. The nearest that one can come at it is to say there are
two--the composed Northern and the impetuous Southern; and both are
found in other countries. Morals? Purity of women may fairly be called
universal with us, but that is the case in some other countries. We have

no monopoly of it; it cannot be named American. I think that there is
but a single specialty with us, only one thing that can be called by the
wide name "American." That is the national devotion to ice-water. All
Germans drink beer, but the British nation drinks beer, too; so neither
of those peoples is the beer-drinking nation. I suppose we do stand
alone in having a drink that nobody likes but ourselves. When we have
been a month in Europe we lose our craving for it, and we finally tell
the hotel folk that they needn't provide it any more. Yet we hardly
touch our native shore again, winter or summer, before we are eager for
it. The reasons for this state of things have not been psychologized
yet. I drop the hint and say no more.

It is my belief that there are some "national" traits and things
scattered about the world that are mere superstitions, frauds that have
lived so long that they have the solid look of facts. One of them is
the dogma that the French are the only chaste people in the world. Ever
since I arrived in France this last time I have been accumulating doubts
about that; and before I leave this sunny land again I will gather in a
few random statistics and psychologize the plausibilities out of it. If
people are to come over to America and find fault with our girls and
our women, and psychologize every little thing they do, and try to teach
them how to behave, and how to cultivate themselves up to where one
cannot tell them from the French model, I intend to find out whether
those missionaries are qualified or not. A nation ought always to
examine into this detail before engaging the teacher for good. This last
one has let fall a remark which renewed those doubts of mine when I read
it:

> "In our high Parisian existence, for instance, we find applied
> to arts and luxury, and to debauchery, all the powers and all
> the weaknesses of the French soul."

You see, it amounts to a trade with the French soul; a profession; a science; the serious business of life, so to speak, in our high Parisian existence. I do not quite like the look of it. I question if it can be taught with profit in our country, except, of course, to those pathetic, neglected minds that are waiting there so yearningly for the education which M. Bourget is going to furnish them from the serene summits of our high Parisian life.

I spoke a moment ago of the existence of some superstitions that have been parading the world as facts this long time. For instance, consider the Dollar. The world seems to think that the love of money is "American"; and that the mad desire to get suddenly rich is "American." I believe that both of these things are merely and broadly human, not American monopolies at all. The love of money is natural to all nations, for money is a good and strong friend. I think that this love has existed everywhere, ever since the Bible called it the root of all evil.

I think that the reason why we Americans seem to be so addicted to trying to get rich suddenly is merely because the opportunity to make promising efforts in that direction has offered itself to us with a frequency out of all proportion to the European experience. For eighty years this opportunity has been offering itself in one new town or region after another straight westward, step by step, all the way from the Atlantic coast to the Pacific. When a mechanic could buy ten town lots on tolerably long credit for ten months' savings out of his wages, and reasonably expect to sell them in a couple of years for ten times what he gave for them, it was human for him to try the venture, and he did it no matter what his nationality was. He would have done it in Europe or China if he had had the same chance.

In the flush times in the silver regions a cook or any other humble worker stood a very good chance to get rich out of a trifle of money risked in a stock deal; and that person promptly took that risk, no matter what his or her nationality might be. I was there, and saw it.

But these opportunities have not been plenty in our Southern States; so there you have a prodigious region where the rush for sudden wealth is almost an unknown thing--and has been, from the beginning.

Europe has offered few opportunities for poor Tom, Dick, and Harry; but when she has offered one, there has been no noticeable difference between European eagerness and American. England saw this in the wild days of the Railroad King; France saw it in 1720--time of Law and the Mississippi Bubble. I am sure I have never seen in the gold and silver mines any madness, fury, frenzy to get suddenly rich which was even remotely comparable to that which raged in France in the Bubble day. If I had a cyclopaedia here I could turn to that memorable case, and satisfy nearly anybody that the hunger for the sudden dollar is no more "American" than it is French. And if I could furnish an American opportunity to staid Germany, I think I could wake her up like a house afire.

But I must return to the Generalizations, Psychologizings, Deductions. When M. Bourget is exploiting these arts, it is then that he is peculiarly and particularly himself. His ways are wholly original when he encounters a trait or a custom which is new to him. Another person would merely examine the find, verify it, estimate its value, and let it go; but that is not sufficient for M. Bourget: he always wants to know why that thing exists, he wants to know how it came to happen; and he will not let go of it until he has found out. And in every instance he will find that reason where no one but himself would have thought of looking for it. He does not seem to care for a reason that is not picturesquely located; one might almost say picturesquely and impossibly located.

He found out that in America men do not try to hunt down young married women. At once, as usual, he wanted to know why. Any one could have told

him. He could have divined it by the lights thrown by the novels of
the country. But no, he preferred to find out for himself. He has a
trustfulness as regards men and facts which is fine and unusual; he is
not particular about the source of a fact, he is not particular about
the character and standing of the fact itself; but when it comes to
pounding out the reason for the existence of the fact, he will trust no
one but himself.

In the present instance here was his fact: American young married women
are not pursued by the corruptor; and here was the question: What is it
that protects her?

It seems quite unlikely that that problem could have offered
difficulties to any but a trained philosopher. Nearly any person would
have said to M. Bourget: "Oh, that is very simple. It is very seldom in
America that a marriage is made on a commercial basis; our marriages,
from the beginning, have been made for love; and where love is there is
no room for the corruptor."

Now, it is interesting to see the formidable way in which M.
Bourget went at that poor, humble little thing. He moved upon it in
column--three columns--and with artillery.

"Two reasons of a very different kind explain"--that fact.

And now that I have got so far, I am almost afraid to say what his
two reasons are, lest I be charged with inventing them. But I will not
retreat now; I will condense them and print them, giving my word that I
am honest and not trying to deceive any one.

1. Young married women are protected from the approaches of the seducer
in New England and vicinity by the diluted remains of a prudence created
by a Puritan law of two hundred years ago, which for a while punished

adultery with death.

2. And young married women of the other forty or fifty States are protected by laws which afford extraordinary facilities for divorce.

If I have not lost my mind I have accurately conveyed those two Vesuvian irruptions of philosophy. But the reader can consult Chapter IV. of 'Outre-Mer', and decide for himself. Let us examine this paralyzing Deduction or Explanation by the light of a few sane facts.

1. This universality of "protection" has existed in our country from the beginning; before the death penalty existed in New England, and during all the generations that have dragged by since it was annulled.

2. Extraordinary facilities for divorce are of such recent creation that any middle-aged American can remember a time when such things had not yet been thought of.

Let us suppose that the first easy divorce law went into effect forty years ago, and got noised around and fairly started in business thirty-five years ago, when we had, say, 25,000,000 of white population. Let us suppose that among 5,000,000 of them the young married women were "protected" by the surviving shudder of that ancient Puritan scare--what is M. Bourget going to do about those who lived among the 20,000,000? They were clean in their morals, they were pure, yet there was no easy divorce law to protect them.

Awhile ago I said that M. Bourget's method of truth-seeking--hunting for it in out-of-the-way places--was new; but that was an error. I remember that when Leverrier discovered the Milky Way, he and the other astronomers began to theorize about it in substantially the same fashion which M. Bourget employs in his seasonings about American social facts and their origin. Leverrier advanced the hypothesis that the Milky

Way was caused by gaseous protoplasmic emanations from the field of Waterloo, which, ascending to an altitude determinable by their own specific gravity, became luminous through the development and exposure--by the natural processes of animal decay--of the phosphorus contained in them.

This theory was warmly complimented by Ptolemy, who, however, after much
thought and research, decided that he could not accept it as final. His own theory was that the Milky Way was an emigration of lightning bugs; and he supported and reinforced this theorem by the well-known fact that the locusts do like that in Egypt.

Giordano Bruno also was outspoken in his praises of Leverrier's important contribution to astronomical science, and was at first inclined to regard it as conclusive; but later, conceiving it to be erroneous, he pronounced against it, and advanced the hypothesis that the Milky Way was a detachment or corps of stars which became arrested and held in 'suspenso suspensorum' by refraction of gravitation while on the march to join their several constellations; a proposition for which he was afterwards burned at the stake in Jacksonville, Illinois.

These were all brilliant and picturesque theories, and each was received with enthusiasm by the scientific world; but when a New England farmer, who was not a thinker, but only a plain sort of person who tried to account for large facts in simple ways, came out with the opinion that the Milky Way was just common, ordinary stars, and was put where it was because God "wanted to hev it so," the admirable idea fell perfectly flat.

As a literary artist, M. Bourget is as fresh and striking as he is as a scientific one. He says, "Above all, I do not believe much in anecdotes."

Why? "In history they are all false"--a sufficiently broad statement--"in literature all libelous"--also a sufficiently sweeping statement, coming from a critic who notes that we are "a people who are peculiarly extravagant in our language--" and when it is a matter of social life, "almost all biased." It seems to amount to stultification, almost. He has built two or three breeds of American coquettes out of anecdotes--mainly "biased" ones, I suppose; and, as they occur "in literature," furnished by his pen, they must be "all libelous." Or did he mean not in literature or anecdotes about literature or literary people? I am not able to answer that. Perhaps the original would be clearer, but I have only the translation of this installment by me. I think the remark had an intention; also that this intention was booked for the trip; but that either in the hurry of the remark's departure it got left, or in the confusion of changing cars at the translator's frontier it got side-tracked.

"But on the other hand I believe in statistics; and those on divorces appear to me to be most conclusive." And he sets himself the task of explaining--in a couple of columns--the process by which Easy-Divorce conceived, invented, originated, developed, and perfected an empire-embracing condition of sexual purity in the States. IN 40 YEARS. No, he doesn't state the interval. With all his passion for statistics he forgot to ask how long it took to produce this gigantic miracle.

I have followed his pleasant but devious trail through those columns, but I was not able to get hold of his argument and find out what it was. I was not even able to find out where it left off. It seemed to gradually dissolve and flow off into other matters. I followed it with interest, for I was anxious to learn how easy-divorce eradicated adultery in America, but I was disappointed; I have no idea yet how it did it. I only know it didn't. But that is not valuable; I knew it before.

Well, humor is the great thing, the saving thing, after all. The minute it crops up, all our hardnesses yield, all our irritations and resentments flit away, and a sunny spirit takes their place. And so, when M. Bourget said that bright thing about our grandfathers, I broke all up. I remember exploding its American countermine once, under that grand hero, Napoleon. He was only First Consul then, and I was Consul-General--for the United States, of course; but we were very intimate, notwithstanding the difference in rank, for I waived that. One day something offered the opening, and he said:

"Well, General, I suppose life can never get entirely dull to an American, because whenever he can't strike up any other way to put in his time he can always get away with a few years trying to find out who his grandfather was!"

I fairly shouted, for I had never heard it sound better; and then I was back at him as quick as a flash--"Right, your Excellency! But I reckon a Frenchman's got his little stand-by for a dull time, too; because when all other interests fail he can turn in and see if he can't find out who his father was!"

Well, you should have heard him just whoop, and cackle, and carry on! He reached up and hit me one on the shoulder, and says:

"Land, but it's good! It's immensely good! George, I never heard it said so good in my life before! Say it again."

So I said it again, and he said his again, and I said mine again, and then he did, and then I did, and then he did, and we kept on doing it, and doing it, and I never had such a good time, and he said the same. In my opinion there isn't anything that is as killing as one of those dear old ripe pensioners if you know how to snatch it out in a kind of a fresh sort of original way.

But I wish M. Bourget had read more of our novels before he came. It is the only way to thoroughly understand a people. When I found I was coming to Paris, I read 'La Terre'.

A LITTLE NOTE TO M. PAUL BOURGET

[The preceding squib was assailed in the North American Review in an article entitled "Mark Twain and Paul Bourget," by Max O'Rell. The following little note is a Rejoinder to that article. It is possible that the position assumed here--that M. Bourget dictated the O'Rell article himself--is untenable.]

You have every right, my dear M. Bourget, to retort upon me by dictation, if you prefer that method to writing at me with your pen; but if I may say it without hurt--and certainly I mean no offence--I believe you would have acquitted yourself better with the pen. With the pen you are at home; it is your natural weapon; you use it with grace, eloquence, charm, persuasiveness, when men are to be convinced, and with formidable effect when they have earned a castigation. But I am sure I see signs in the above article that you are either unaccustomed to dictating or are out of practice. If you will re-read it you will notice, yourself, that it lacks definiteness; that it lacks purpose; that it lacks coherence; that it lacks a subject to talk about; that it is loose and wabbly; that it wanders around; that it loses itself early and does not find itself any more. There are some other defects, as you will notice, but I think I have named the main ones. I feel sure that they are all due to your lack of practice in dictating.

Inasmuch as you had not signed it I had the impression at first that you had not dictated it. But only for a moment. Certain quite simple and definite facts reminded me that the article had to come from you, for the reason that it could not come from any one else without a specific invitation from you or from me. I mean, it could not except as an intrusion, a transgression of the law which forbids strangers to mix into a private dispute between friends, unasked.

Those simple and definite facts were these: I had published an article in this magazine, with you for my subject; just you yourself; I stuck strictly to that one subject, and did not interlard any other. No one, of course, could call me to account but you alone, or your authorized representative. I asked some questions--asked them of myself. I answered them myself. My article was thirteen pages long, and all devoted to you; devoted to you, and divided up in this way: one page of guesses as to what subjects you would instruct us in, as teacher; one page of doubts as to the effectiveness of your method of examining us and our ways; two or three pages of criticism of your method, and of certain results which it furnished you; two or three pages of attempts to show the justness of these same criticisms; half a dozen pages made up of slight fault-findings with certain minor details of your literary workmanship, of extracts from your 'Outre-Mer' and comments upon them; then I closed with an anecdote. I repeat--for certain reasons--that I closed with an anecdote.

When I was asked by this magazine if I wished to "answer" a "reply" to that article of mine, I said "yes," and waited in Paris for the proof-sheets of the "reply" to come. I already knew, by the cablegram, that the "reply" would not be signed by you, but upon reflection I knew it would be dictated by you, because no volunteer would feel himself at liberty to assume your championship in a private dispute, unasked,

in view of the fact that you are quite well able to take care of your
matters of that sort yourself and are not in need of any one's help.
No, a volunteer could not make such a venture. It would be too immodest.
Also too gratuitously generous. And a shade too self-sufficient. No, he
could not venture it. It would look too much like anxiety to get in at a
feast where no plate had been provided for him. In fact he could not get
in at all, except by the back way, and with a false key; that is to say,
a pretext--a pretext invented for the occasion by putting into my mouth
words which I did not use, and by wresting sayings of mine from their
plain and true meaning. Would he resort to methods like those to get
in? No; there are no people of that kind. So then I knew for a certainty
that you dictated the Reply yourself. I knew you did it to save yourself
manual labor.

And you had the right, as I have already said and I am
content--perfectly content.

Yet it would have been little trouble to you, and a great kindness to
me, if you had written your Reply all out with your own capable hand.

Because then it would have replied--and that is really what a Reply is
for. Broadly speaking, its function is to refute--as you will easily
concede. That leaves something for the other person to take hold of:
he has a chance to reply to the Reply, he has a chance to refute the
refutation. This would have happened if you had written it out instead
of dictating. Dictating is nearly sure to unconcentrate the dictator's
mind, when he is out of practice, confuse him, and betray him into using
one set of literary rules when he ought to use a quite different set.
Often it betrays him into employing the RULES FOR CONVERSATION
BETWEEN A SHOUTER AND A DEAF PERSON--as in the present case--
when he ought to employ the RULES FOR CONDUCTING DISCUSSION WITH A
FAULT-FINDER. The great foundation-rule and basic principle of discussion with
a fault-finder is relevancy and concentration upon the subject; whereas

the great foundation-rule and basic principle governing conversation between a shouter and a deaf person is irrelevancy and persistent desertion of the topic in hand. If I may be allowed to illustrate by quoting example IV., section from chapter ix. of "Revised Rules for Conducting Conversation between a Shouter and a Deaf Person," it will assist us in getting a clear idea of the difference between the two sets of rules:

Shouter. Did you say his name is WETHERBY?

Deaf Person. Change? Yes, I think it will. Though if it should clear off I--

Shouter. It's his NAME I want--his NAME.

Deaf Person. Maybe so, maybe so; but it will only be a shower, I think.

Shouter. No, no, no!--you have quite misunderSTOOD me. If--

Deaf Person. Ah! GOOD morning; I am sorry you must go. But call again, and let me continue to be of assistance to you in every way I can.

You see it is a perfect kodak of the article you have dictated. It is really curious and interesting when you come to compare it with yours; in detail, with my former article to which it is a Reply in your hand. I talk twelve pages about your American instruction projects, and your doubtful scientific system, and your painstaking classification of nonexistent things, and your diligence and zeal and sincerity, and your disloyal attitude towards anecdotes, and your undue reverence for unsafe statistics and far facts that lack a pedigree; and you turn around and come back at me with eight pages of weather.

I do not see how a person can act so. It is good of you to repeat, with change of language, in the bulk of your rejoinder, so much of my own article, and adopt my sentiments, and make them over, and put new buttons on; and I like the compliment, and am frank to say so; but agreeing with a person cripples controversy and ought not to be allowed. It is weather; and of almost the worst sort. It pleases me greatly to hear you discourse with such approval and expansiveness upon my text:

"A foreigner can photograph the exteriors of a nation, but I think that is as far as he can get. I think that no foreigner can report its interior;"--[And you say: "A man of average intelligence, who has passed six months among a people, cannot express opinions that are worth jotting down, but he can form impressions that are worth repeating. For my part, I think that foreigners' impressions are more interesting than native opinions. After all, such impressions merely mean 'how the country struck the foreigner.'"]--which is a quite clear way of saying that a foreigner's report is only valuable when it restricts itself to impressions. It pleases me to have you follow my lead in that glowing way, but it leaves me nothing to combat. You should give me something to deny and refute; I would do as much for you.

It pleases me to have you playfully warn the public against taking one of your books seriously.--[When I published Jonathan and his Continent, I wrote in a preface addressed to Jonathan: "If ever you should insist in seeing in this little volume a serious study of your country and of your countrymen, I warn you that your world-wide fame for humor will be exploded."]--Because I used to do that cunning thing myself in earlier days. I did it in a prefatory note to a book of mine called Tom Sawyer.

NOTICE.

Persons attempting to find a motive in

this narrative will be prosecuted;
persons attempting to find a moral in it
will be banished; persons attempting to
find a plot in it will be shot.
   BY ORDER OF THE AUTHOR
   PER G. G., CHIEF OF ORDNANCE.

The kernel is the same in both prefaces, you see--the public must
not take us too seriously. If we remove that kernel we remove the
life-principle, and the preface is a corpse. Yes, it pleases me to have
you use that idea, for it is a high compliment. But is leaves me nothing
to combat; and that is damage to me.

Am I seeming to say that your Reply is not a reply at all, M. Bourget?
If so, I must modify that; it is too sweeping. For you have furnished
a general answer to my inquiry as to what France through you--can teach
us.--["What could France teach America!" exclaims Mark Twain. France
can teach America all the higher pursuits of life, and there is more
artistic feeling and refinement in a street of French workingmen than in
many avenues inhabited by American millionaires. She can teach her, not
perhaps how to work, but how to rest, how to live, how to be happy.
She can teach her that the aim of life is not money-making, but that
money-making is only a means to obtain an end. She can teach her
that wives are not expensive toys, but useful partners, friends, and
confidants, who should always keep men under their wholesome
influence by their diplomacy, their tact, their common-sense, without
bumptiousness. These qualities, added to the highest standard of
morality (not angular and morose, but cheerful morality), are conceded
to Frenchwomen by whoever knows something of French life outside of the
Paris boulevards, and Mark Twain's ill-natured sneer cannot even so much
as stain them.

I might tell Mark Twain that in France a man who was seen tipsy in his club would immediately see his name canceled from membership. A man who had settled his fortune on his wife to avoid meeting his creditors would be refused admission into any decent society. Many a Frenchman has blown his brains out rather than declare himself a bankrupt. Now would Mark Twain remark to this: 'An American is not such a fool: when a creditor stands in his way he closes his doors, and reopens them the following day. When he has been a bankrupt three times he can retire from business?']--It is a good answer.

It relates to manners, customs, and morals--three things concerning which we can never have exhaustive and determinate statistics, and so the verdicts delivered upon them must always lack conclusiveness and be subject to revision; but you have stated the truth, possibly, as nearly as any one could do it, in the circumstances. But why did you choose a detail of my question which could be answered only with vague hearsay evidence, and go right by one which could have been answered with deadly facts?--facts in everybody's reach, facts which none can dispute. I asked what France could teach us about government. I laid myself pretty wide open, there; and I thought I was handsomely generous, too, when I did it. France can teach us how to levy village and city taxes which distribute the burden with a nearer approach to perfect fairness than is the case in any other land; and she can teach us the wisest and surest system of collecting them that exists. She can teach us how to elect a President in a sane way; and also how to do it without throwing the country into earthquakes and convulsions that cripple and embarrass business, stir up party hatred in the hearts of men, and make peaceful people wish the term extended to thirty years. France can teach us--but enough of that part of the question. And what else can France teach us? She can teach us all the fine arts--and does. She throws open her hospitable art academies, and says to us, "Come"--and we come, troops and troops of our young and gifted; and she sets over us the ablest masters in the world and bearing the greatest names; and she, teaches us all that we are capable of learning, and persuades us and encourages us with prizes and honors, much as if we were somehow children of her own; and when this noble education is finished and we are ready to carry it home and spread its gracious ministries abroad over our nation, and we come with homage and gratitude and ask France for the bill--there is nothing to pay. And in return for this imperial generosity, what does America do? She charges a duty on French works of art!

I wish I had your end of this dispute; I should have something worth talking about. If you would only furnish me something to argue, something to refute--but you persistently won't. You leave good chances unutilized and spend your strength in proving and establishing unimportant things. For instance, you have proven and established these eight facts here following--a good score as to number, but not worth while:

Mark Twain is--

1. "Insulting."

2. (Sarcastically speaking) "This refined humor, 1st."

3. Prefers the manure-pile to the violets.

4. Has uttered "an ill-natured sneer."

5. Is "nasty."

6. Needs a "lesson in politeness and good manners."

7. Has published a "nasty article."

8. Has made remarks "unworthy of a gentleman."--["It is more funny than

his" (Mark Twain's) "anecdote, and would have been less insulting."]

A quoted remark of mine "is a gross insult to a nation friendly to America."

"He has read La Terre, this refined humorist."

"When Mark Twain visits a garden... he goes in the far-away corner where the soil is prepared."

"Mark Twain's ill-natured sneer cannot so much as stain them" (the Frenchwomen).

"When he" (Mark Twain) "takes his revenge he is unkind, unfair, bitter, nasty."

"But not even your nasty article on my country, Mark," etc.

"Mark might certainly have derived from it" (M. Bourget's book) "a lesson in politeness and good manners."

A quoted remark of mine is "unworthy of a gentleman."--

These are all true, but really they are not valuable; no one cares much for such finds. In our American magazines we recognize this and suppress them. We avoid naming them. American writers never allow themselves to name them. It would look as if they were in a temper, and we hold that exhibitions of temper in public are not good form except in the very young and inexperienced. And even if we had the disposition to name them, in order to fill up a gap when we were short of ideas and arguments, our magazines would not allow us to do it, because they think that such words sully their pages. This present magazine is particularly strenuous about it. Its note to me announcing the forwarding of your proof-sheets to France closed thus--for your protection:

"It is needless to ask you to avoid anything that he might consider as personal."

It was well enough, as a measure of precaution, but really it was not needed. You can trust me implicitly, M. Bourget; I shall never call you any names in print which I should be ashamed to call you with your unoffending and dearest ones present.

Indeed, we are reserved, and particular in America to a degree which you would consider exaggerated. For instance, we should not write notes like that one of yours to a lady for a small fault--or a large one.--[When M. Paul Bourget indulges in a little chaffing at the expense of the Americans, "who can always get away with a few years' trying to find out who their grandfathers were,"] he merely makes an allusion to an American foible; but, forsooth, what a kind man, what a humorist Mark Twain is when he retorts by calling France a nation of bastards! How the Americans of culture and refinement will admire him for thus speaking in their name!

Snobbery.... I could give Mark Twain an example of the American specimen. It is a piquant story. I never published it because I feared my readers might think that I was giving them a typical illustration of American character instead of a rare exception.

I was once booked by my manager to give a causerie in the drawing-room of a New York millionaire. I accepted with reluctance. I do not like private engagements. At five o'clock on the day the causerie was to be given, the lady sent to my manager to say that she would expect me to arrive at nine o'clock and to speak for about an hour. Then she wrote a postscript. Many women are unfortunate there. Their minds are full of after-thoughts, and the most important part of their letters is generally to be found after their signature. This lady's P. S. ran thus: "I suppose he will not expect to be entertained after the lecture."

I fairly shorted, as Mark Twain would say, and then, indulging myself in a bit of snobbishness, I was back at her as quick as a flash:

"Dear Madam: As a literary man of some reputation, I have many times had the pleasure of being entertained by the members of the old aristocracy of France. I have also many times had the pleasure of being entertained by the members of the old aristocracy of England. If it may interest you, I can even tell you that I have several times had the honor of being entertained by royalty; but my ambition has never been so wild as to expect that one day I might be entertained by the aristocracy of New York. No, I do not expect to be entertained by you, nor do I want you to expect me to entertain you and your friends to-night, for I decline to keep the engagement."

Now, I could fill a book on America with reminiscences of this sort, adding a few chapters on bosses and boodlers, on New York 'chronique scandaleuse', on the tenement houses of the large cities, on the gambling-hells of Denver, and the dens of San Francisco, and what not! [But not even your nasty article on my country, Mark, will make me do it.]--We should not think it kind. No matter how much we might have associated with kings and nobilities, we should not think it right to crush her with it and make her ashamed of her lowlier walk in life; for we have a saying, "Who humiliates my mother includes his own."

Do I seriously imagine you to be the author of that strange letter, M. Bourget? Indeed I do not. I believe it to have been surreptitiously inserted by your amanuensis when your back was turned. I think he did it with a good motive, expecting it to add force and piquancy to your article, but it does not reflect your nature, and I know it will grieve you when you see it. I also think he interlarded many other things which you will disapprove of when you see them. I am certain that all the harsh names discharged at me come from him, not you. No doubt you could have proved me entitled to them with as little trouble as it has cost him to do it, but it would have been your disposition to hunt game of a higher quality.

Why, I even doubt if it is you who furnish me all that excellent information about Balzac and those others.--["Now the style of M. Bourget and many other French writers is apparently a closed letter to Mark Twain; but let us leave that alone. Has he read Erckmann-Chatrian, Victor Hugo, Lamartine, Edmond About, Cherbuliez, Renan? Has he read Gustave Droz's 'Monsieur, Madame, et Bebe', and those books which leave for a long time a perfume about you? Has he read the novels of Alexandre Dumas, Eugene Sue, George Sand, and Balzac? Has he read Victor Hugo's 'Les Miserables' and 'Notre Dame de Paris'? Has he read or heard the plays of Sandeau, Augier, Dumas, and Sardou, the works of those Titans of modern literature, whose names will be household words all over the world for hundreds of years to come? He has read La Terre--this kind-hearted, refined humorist! When Mark Twain visits a garden does he smell the violets, the roses, the jasmine, or the honeysuckle? No, he goes in the far-away corner where the soil is prepared. Hear what he says: 'I wish M. Paul Bourget had read more of our novels before he came. It is the only way to thoroughly understand a people. When I found I was coming to Paris I read La Terre.'"]--All this in simple justice to you--and to me; for, to gravely accept those interlardings as yours would be to wrong your head and heart, and at the same time convict myself of being equipped with a vacancy where my penetration ought to be lodged.

And now finally I must uncover the secret pain, the wee sore from which the Reply grew--the anecdote which closed my recent article--and consider how it is that this pimple has spread to these cancerous dimensions. If any but you had dictated the Reply, M. Bourget, I would know that that anecdote was twisted around and its intention magnified some hundreds of times, in order that it might be used as a pretext to creep in the back way. But I accuse you of nothing--nothing but error. When you say that I "retort by calling France a nation of bastards," it is an error. And not a small one, but a large one. I made no such remark, nor anything resembling it. Moreover, the magazine would not have allowed me to use so gross a word as that.

You told an anecdote. A funny one--I admit that. It hit a foible of our American aristocracy, and it stung me--I admit that; it stung me sharply. It was like this: You found some ancient portraits of French kings in the gallery of one of our aristocracy, and you said:

"He has the Grand Monarch, but where is the portrait of his grandfather?" That is, the American aristocrat's grandfather.

Now that hits only a few of us, I grant--just the upper crust only--but it hits exceedingly hard.

I wondered if there was any way of getting back at you. In one of your chapters I found this chance:

"In our high Parisian existence, for instance, we find applied to arts and luxury, and to debauchery, all the powers and all the weaknesses of the French soul."

You see? Your "higher Parisian" class--not everybody, not the nation, but only the top crust of the Ovation--applies to debauchery all the powers of its soul.

I argued to myself that that energy must produce results. So I built an anecdote out of your remark. In it I make Napoleon Bonaparte say to me--but see for yourself the anecdote (ingeniously clipped and curtailed) in paragraph eleven of your Reply.--[So, I repeat, Mark Twain does not like M. Paul Bourget's book. So long as he makes light fun of the great French writer he is at home, he is pleasant, he is the American humorist we know. When he takes his revenge (and where is the reason for taking a revenge?) he is unkind, unfair, bitter, nasty.]

For example: See his answer to a Frenchman who jokingly remarks to him:

"I suppose life can never get entirely dull to an American, because whenever he can't strike up any other way to put in his time, he can always get away with a few years trying to find out who his grandfather was."

Hear the answer:

"I reckon a Frenchman's got his little standby for a dull time, too; because when all other interests fail, he can turn in and see if he can't find out who his father was."

The first remark is a good-humored bit of chaffing on American snobbery. I may be utterly destitute of humor, but I call the second remark a gratuitous charge of immorality hurled at the French women--a remark unworthy of a man who has the ear of the public, unworthy of a gentleman, a gross insult to a nation friendly to America, a nation that helped Mark Twain's ancestors in their struggle for liberty, a nation where to-day it is enough to say that you are American to see every door open wide to you.

If Mark Twain was hard up in search of, a French "chestnut," I might have told him the following little anecdote. It is more funny than his, and would have been less insulting: Two little street boys are abusing each other. "Ah, hold your tongue," says one, "you ain't got no father."

"Ain't got no father!" replies the other; "I've got more fathers than you."

Now, then, your anecdote about the grandfathers hurt me. Why? Because it had a point. It wouldn't have hurt me if it hadn't had point. You wouldn't have wasted space on it if it hadn't had point.

My anecdote has hurt you. Why? Because it had point, I suppose. It wouldn't have hurt you if it hadn't had point. I judged from your remark about the diligence and industry of the high Parisian upper crust that it would have some point, but really I had no idea what a gold-mine I had struck. I never suspected that the point was going to stick into the entire nation; but of course you know your nation better than I do, and if you think it punctures them all, I have to yield to your judgment. But you are to blame, your own self. Your remark misled me. I supposed the industry was confined to that little unnumerous upper layer.

Well, now that the unfortunate thing has been done, let us do what we can to undo it. There must be a way, M. Bourget, and I am willing to do anything that will help; for I am as sorry as you can be yourself.

I will tell you what I think will be the very thing.

We will swap anecdotes. I will take your anecdote and you take mine. I will say to the dukes and counts and princes of the ancient nobility of France:

"Ha, ha! You must have a pretty hard time trying to find out who your grandfathers were?"

They will merely smile indifferently and not feel hurt, because they can trace their lineage back through centuries.

And you will hurl mine at every individual in the American nation, saying:

"And you must have a pretty hard time trying to find out who your fathers were." They will merely smile indifferently, and not feel hurt, because they haven't any difficulty in finding their fathers.

Do you get the idea? The whole harm in the anecdotes is in the point, you see; and when we swap them around that way, they haven't any.

That settles it perfectly and beautifully, and I am glad I thought of it. I am very glad indeed, M. Bourget; for it was just that little wee thing that caused the whole difficulty and made you dictate the Reply, and your amanuensis call me all those hard names which the magazines dislike so. And I did it all in fun, too, trying to cap your funny anecdote with another one--on the give-and-take principle, you know--which is American. I didn't know that with the French it was all give and no take, and you didn't tell me. But now that I have made everything comfortable again, and fixed both anecdotes so they can never have any point any more, I know you will forgive me.

www.bookjungle.com *email: sales@bookjungle.com fax: 630-214-0564 mail: Book Jungle PO Box 2226 Champaign, IL 61825*

The Codes Of Hammurabi And Moses
W. W. Davies

QTY

The discovery of the Hammurabi Code is one of the greatest achievements of archaeology, and is of paramount interest, not only to the student of the Bible, but also to all those interested in ancient history...

Religion   **ISBN:** *1-59462-338-4*   **Pages:132**
MSRP $12.95

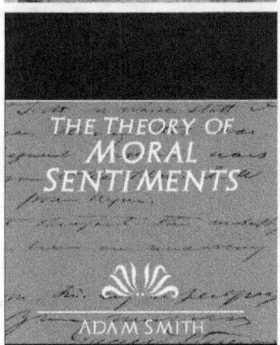

The Theory of Moral Sentiments
Adam Smith

QTY

This work from 1749. contains original theories of conscience amd moral judgment and it is the foundation for systemof morals.

Philosophy ISBN: *1-59462-777-0*   **Pages:536**
MSRP $19.95

Jessica's First Prayer
Hesba Stretton

QTY

In a screened and secluded corner of one of the many railway-bridges which span the streets of London there could be seen a few years ago, from five o'clock every morning until half past eight, a tidily set-out coffee-stall, consisting of a trestle and board, upon which stood two large tin cans, with a small fire of charcoal burning under each so as to keep the coffee boiling during the early hours of the morning when the work-people were thronging into the city on their way to their daily toil...

Pages:84

Childrens   ISBN: *1-59462-373-2*   *MSRP $9.95*

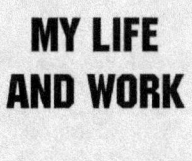

My Life and Work
Henry Ford

QTY

Henry Ford revolutionized the world with his implementation of mass production for the Model T automobile. Gain valuable business insight into his life and work with his own auto-biography... "We have only started on our development of our country we have not as yet, with all our talk of wonderful progress, done more than scratch the surface. The progress has been wonderful enough but..."

Pages:300

Biographies/   ISBN: *1-59462-198-5*   *MSRP $21.95*

www.bookjungle.com *email: sales@bookjungle.com fax: 630-214-0564 mail: Book Jungle PO Box 2226 Champaign, IL 61825*

The Art of Cross-Examination
Francis Wellman

QTY

I presume it is the experience of every author, after his first book is published upon an important subject, to be almost overwhelmed with a wealth of ideas and illustrations which could readily have been included in his book, and which to his own mind, at least, seem to make a second edition inevitable. Such certainly was the case with me; and when the first edition had reached its sixth impression in five months, I rejoiced to learn that it seemed to my publishers that the book had met with a sufficiently favorable reception to justify a second and considerably enlarged edition. ..

Pages:412

Reference   **ISBN: *1-59462-647-2***   *MSRP $19.95*

On the Duty of Civil Disobedience
Henry David Thoreau

QTY

Thoreau wrote his famous essay, On the Duty of Civil Disobedience, as a protest against an unjust but popular war and the immoral but popular institution of slave-owning. He did more than write—he declined to pay his taxes, and was hauled off to gaol in consequence. Who can say how much this refusal of his hastened the end of the war and of slavery ?

Law   **ISBN: *1-59462-747-9***   **Pages:48**

MSRP $7.45

Dream Psychology Psychoanalysis for Beginners
Sigmund Freud

QTY

Sigmund Freud, born Sigismund Schlomo Freud (May 6, 1856 - September 23, 1939), was a Jewish-Austrian neurologist and psychiatrist who co-founded the psychoanalytic school of psychology. Freud is best known for his theories of the unconscious mind, especially involving the mechanism of repression; his redefinition of sexual desire as mobile and directed towards a wide variety of objects; and his therapeutic techniques, especially his understanding of transference in the therapeutic relationship and the presumed value of dreams as sources of insight into unconscious desires.

Pages:196

Psychology   **ISBN: *1-59462-905-6***   *MSRP $15.45*

The Miracle of Right Thought
Orison Swett Marden

QTY

Believe with all of your heart that you will do what you were made to do. When the mind has once formed the habit of holding cheerful, happy, prosperous pictures, it will not be easy to form the opposite habit. It does not matter how improbable or how far away this realization may see, or how dark the prospects may be, if we visualize them as best we can, as vividly as possible, hold tenaciously to them and vigorously struggle to attain them, they will gradually become actualized, realized in the life. But a desire, a longing without endeavor, a yearning abandoned or held indifferently will vanish without realization.

Pages:360

Self Help   **ISBN: *1-59462-644-8***   *MSRP $25.45*

QTY

The Rosicrucian Cosmo-Conception Mystic Christianity *by Max Heindel*   ISBN: *1-59462-188-8* **$38.95**
The Rosicrucian Cosmo-conception is not dogmatic, neither does it appeal to any other authority than the reason of the student. It is: not controversial, but is: sent forth in the, hope that it may help to clear...   *New Age/Religion Pages 646*

Abandonment To Divine Providence *by Jean-Pierre de Caussade*   ISBN: *1-59462-228-0* **$25.95**
"The Rev. Jean Pierre de Caussade was one of the most remarkable spiritual writers of the Society of Jesus in France in the 18th Century. His death took place at Toulouse in 1751. His works have gone through many editions and have been republished...   *Inspirational/Religion Pages 400*

Mental Chemistry *by Charles Haanel*   ISBN: *1-59462-192-6* **$23.95**
Mental Chemistry allows the change of material conditions by combining and appropriately utilizing the power of the mind. Much like applied chemistry creates something new and unique out of careful combinations of chemicals the mastery of mental chemistry...   *New Age Pages 354*

The Letters of Robert Browning and Elizabeth Barret Barrett 1845-1846 vol II   ISBN: *1-59462-193-4* **$35.95**
by Robert Browning and Elizabeth Barrett   *Biographies Pages 596*

Gleanings In Genesis (volume I) *by Arthur W. Pink*   ISBN: *1-59462-130-6* **$27.45**
Appropriately has Genesis been termed "the seed plot of the Bible" for in it we have, in germ form, almost all of the great doctrines which are afterwards fully developed in the books of Scripture which follow...   *Religion/Inspirational Pages 420*

The Master Key *by L. W. de Laurence*   ISBN: *1-59462-001-6* **$30.95**
In no branch of human knowledge has there been a more lively increase of the spirit of research during the past few years than in the study of Psychology, Concentration and Mental Discipline. The requests for authentic lessons in Thought Control, Mental Discipline and...   *New Age/Business Pages 422*

The Lesser Key Of Solomon Goetia *by L. W. de Laurence*   ISBN: *1-59462-092-X* **$9.95**
This translation of the first book of the "Lernegton" which is now for the first time made accessible to students of Talismanic Magic was from, after careful collation and edition, from numerous Ancient Manuscripts in Hebrew, Latin, and French...   *New Age/Occult Pages 92*

Rubaiyat Of Omar Khayyam *by Edward Fitzgerald*   ISBN:*1-59462-332-5* **$13.95**
Edward Fitzgerald, whom the world has already learned, in spite of his own efforts to remain within the shadow of anonymity, to look upon as one of the rarest poets of the century, was born at Bredfield, in Suffolk, on the 31st of March, 1809. He was the third son of John Purcell...   *Music Pages 172*

Ancient Law *by Henry Maine*   ISBN: *1-59462-128-4* **$29.95**
The chief object of the following pages is to indicate some of the earliest ideas of mankind, as they are reflected in Ancient Law, and to point out the relation of those ideas to modern thought.   *Religiom/History Pages 452*

Far-Away Stories *by William J. Locke*   ISBN: *1-59462-129-2* **$19.45**
"Good wine needs no bush, but a collection of mixed vintages does. And this book is just such a collection. Some of the stories I do not want to remain buried for ever in the museum files of dead magazine-numbers an author's not unpardonable vanity..."   *Fiction Pages 272*

Life of David Crockett *by David Crockett*   ISBN: *1-59462-250-7* **$27.45**
"Colonel David Crockett was one of the most remarkable men of the times in which he lived. Born in humble life, but gifted with a strong will, an indomitable courage, and unremitting perseverance...   *Biographies/New Age Pages 424*

Lip-Reading *by Edward Nitchie*   ISBN: *1-59462-206-X* **$25.95**
Edward B. Nitchie, founder of the New York School for the Hard of Hearing, now the Nitchie School of Lip-Reading, Inc, wrote "LIP-READING Principles and Practice". The development and perfecting of this meritorious work on lip-reading was an undertaking...   *How-to Pages 400*

A Handbook of Suggestive Therapeutics, Applied Hypnotism, Psychic Science   ISBN: *1-59462-214-0* **$24.95**
by Henry Munro   *Health/New Age/Health/Self-help Pages 376*

A Doll's House: and Two Other Plays *by Henrik Ibsen*   ISBN: *1-59462-112-8* **$19.95**
Henrik Ibsen created this classic when in revolutionary 1848 Rome. Introducing some striking concepts in playwriting for the realist genre, this play has been studied the world over.   *Fiction/Classics/Plays 308*

The Light of Asia *by sir Edwin Arnold*   ISBN: *1-59462-204-3* **$13.95**
In this poetic masterpiece, Edwin Arnold describes the life and teachings of Buddha. The man who was to become known as Buddha to the world was born as Prince Gautama of India but he rejected the worldly riches and abandoned the reigns of power when... *Religion/History/Biographies Pages 170*

The Complete Works of Guy de Maupassant *by Guy de Maupassant*   ISBN: *1-59462-157-8* **$16.95**
"For days and days, nights and nights, I had dreamed of that first kiss which was to consecrate our engagement, and I knew not on what spot I should put my lips..."   *Fiction/Classics Pages 240*

The Art of Cross-Examination *by Francis L. Wellman*   ISBN: *1-59462-309-0* **$26.95**
Written by a renowned trial lawyer, Wellman imparts his experience and uses case studies to explain how to use psychology to extract desired information through questioning.   *How-to/Science/Reference Pages 408*

Answered or Unanswered? *by Louisa Vaughan*   ISBN: *1-59462-248-5* **$10.95**
Miracles of Faith in China   *Religion Pages 112*

The Edinburgh Lectures on Mental Science (1909) *by Thomas*   ISBN: *1-59462-008-3* **$11.95**
This book contains the substance of a course of lectures recently given by the writer in the Queen Street Hail, Edinburgh. Its purpose is to indicate the Natural Principles governing the relation between Mental Action and Material Conditions...   *New Age/Psychology Pages 148*

Ayesha *by H. Rider Haggard*   ISBN: *1-59462-301-5* **$24.95**
Verily and indeed it is the unexpected that happens! Probably if there was one person upon the earth from whom the Editor of this, and of a certain previous history, did not expect to hear again...   *Classics Pages 380*

Ayala's Angel *by Anthony Trollope*   ISBN: *1-59462-352-X* **$29.95**
The two girls were both pretty, but Lucy who was twenty-one who supposed to be simple and comparatively unattractive, whereas Ayala was credited, as her Bombwhat romantic name might show, with poetic charm and a taste for romance. Ayala when her father died was nineteen...   *Fiction Pages 484*

The American Commonwealth *by James Bryce*   ISBN: *1-59462-286-8* **$34.45**
An interpretation of American democratic political theory. It examines political mechanics and society from the perspective of Scotsman James Bryce   *Politics Pages 572*

Stories of the Pilgrims *by Margaret P. Pumphrey*   ISBN: *1-59462-116-0* **$17.95**
This book explores pilgrims religious oppression in England as well as their escape to Holland and eventual crossing to America on the Mayflower, and their early days in New England...   *History Pages 268*

QTY

The Fasting Cure *by Sinclair Upton*　　　　　　　　　　　　　　ISBN: *1-59462-222-1*　**$13.95**
In the Cosmopolitan Magazine for May, 1910, and in the Contemporary Review (London) for April, 1910, I published an article dealing with my experi-
ences in fasting. I have written a great many magazine articles, but never one which attracted so much attention... New Age/Self Help/Health Pages 164

☐

Hebrew Astrology *by Sepharial*　　　　　　　　　　　　　　　ISBN: *1-59462-308-2*　**$13.45**
In these days of advanced thinking it is a matter of common observation that we have left many of the old landmarks behind and that we are now pressing
forward to greater heights and to a wider horizon than that which represented the mind-content of our progenitors...　　　Astrology Pages 144

☐

Thought Vibration or The Law of Attraction in the Thought World　　ISBN: *1-59462-127-6*　**$12.95**

by William Walker Atkinson　　　　　　　　　　　　　　　　　　　　Psychology/Religion Pages 144

☐

Optimism *by Helen Keller*　　　　　　　　　　　　　　　　　ISBN: *1-59462-108-X*　**$15.95**
Helen Keller was blind, deaf, and mute since 19 months old, yet famously learned how to overcome these handicaps, communicate with the world, and
spread her lectures promoting optimism. An inspiring read for everyone...　　　　Biographies/Inspirational Pages 84

☐

Sara Crewe *by Frances Burnett*　　　　　　　　　　　　　　　ISBN: *1-59462-360-0*　**$9.45**
In the first place, Miss Minchin lived in London. Her home was a large, dull, tall one, in a large, dull square, where all the houses were alike, and all the
sparrows were alike, and where all the door-knockers made the same heavy sound...　　　Childrens/Classic Pages 88

☐

The Autobiography of Benjamin Franklin *by Benjamin Franklin*　　　ISBN: *1-59462-135-7*　**$24.95**
The Autobiography of Benjamin Franklin has probably been more extensively read than any other American historical work, and no other book of its kind
has had such ups and downs of fortune. Franklin lived for many years in England, where he was agent...　　　Biographies/History Pages 332

☐

Name	
Email	
Telephone	
Address	
City, State ZIP	

☐ **Credit Card**　　　　　　　☐ **Check / Money Order**

Credit Card Number	
Expiration Date	
Signature	

Please Mail to:　Book Jungle
PO Box 2226
Champaign, IL 61825
or Fax to:　　630-214-0564

ORDERING INFORMATION

web*: www.bookjungle.com*
email*: sales@bookjungle.com*
fax*: 630-214-0564*
mail*: Book Jungle PO Box 2226 Champaign, IL 61825*
or PayPal *to sales@bookjungle.com*

Please contact us for bulk discounts

DIRECT-ORDER TERMS

20% Discount if You Order
Two or More Books
Free Domestic Shipping!
Accepted: Master Card, Visa,
Discover, American Express

www.ingramcontent.com/pod-product-compliance
Lightning Source LLC
Chambersburg PA
CBHW082018170626
46817CB00009B/3133